For Mom, Dad, Kathleen, and Jimmy—

Thank you for supporting all of my Buckeye adventures.

Go Bucks!

www.mascotbooks.com

There Once Was a Buckeye Who Lived in The Shoe.

For more information, please contact:
Mascot Books
620 Herndon Parkway #320
Herndon, VA 20170
info@mascotbooks.com

CPSIA Code: PRT0618A
ISBN-13: 978-1-63177-869-8

Printed in the United States

There Once Was a Buckeye Who Lived in The Shoe.®

written by **Stephanie Duwve**

illustrated by Giada Guidice

There once was a Buckeye who lived in The Shoe,
He had so many friends he didn't know what to do.

Some lived near and some lived far.

They came to visit by bus, plane, or car.

They came mostly on Saturdays, at night time or day,

To cheer on the Buckeyes and watch the team play.

That team up north, they're our friends, too.

We love when they come to visit The Shoe.

While inside The Shoe,
you'll hear "O-H-I-O"

And cheers for our
quarterback to make a
great throw.

The coach tells the team the plays they should run.

We win some, we lose some, but we always have fun.

They work hard together as good teammates do.

Woody taught them that lesson long ago in The Shoe.

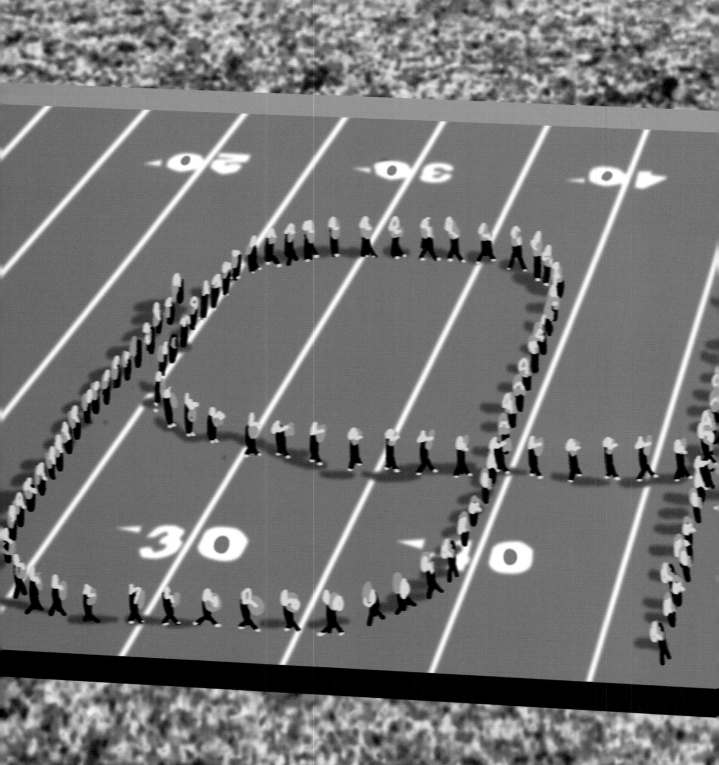

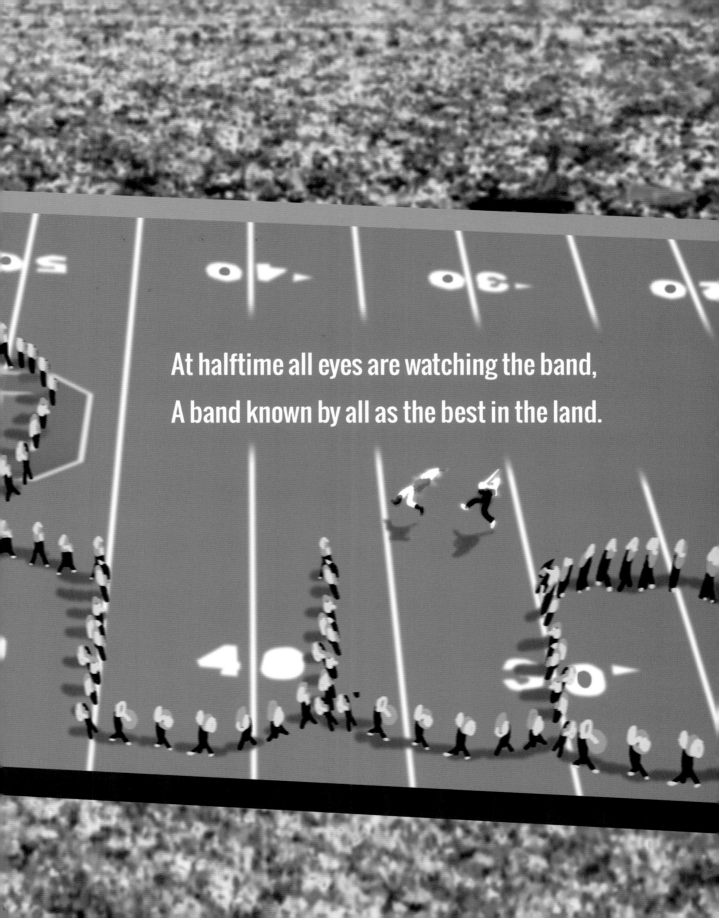

At halftime all eyes are watching the band,
A band known by all as the best in the land.

Singing "Hang on Sloopy" or dotting the i,

Traditions are
loved when
you're a Buckeye.

When the last play is through and time runs out,

We link arms and sing "Carmen," that's what friendship's about.

The state of Ohio is a great place to be.

Our Buckeyes play hard for you and for me.

So, if you wear scarlet and gray and visit The Shoe,

Maybe one day you'll be a Buckeye, too!

Carmen Ohio

Oh! Come let's sing Ohio's praise,
And songs to Alma Mater raise;
While our hearts rebounding thrill,
With joy which death alone can still.
Summer's heat or Winter's cold,
The seasons pass, the years will roll;
Time and change will surely show
How firm thy friendship O-hi-o.

Across the Field

Fight the team across the field,
Show them Ohio's here
Set the earth reverberating with
a mighty cheer
Rah! Rah! Rah!
Hit them hard and see how they fall;
Never let that team get the ball,
Hail! Hail! The gang's all here,
So let's win that old conference now.

Buckeye Battle Cry

In old Ohio there's a team
That's known thru-out the land;
Eleven warriors, brave and bold,
Whose fame will ever stand.
And when the ball goes over,
Our cheers will reach the sky,
Ohio field will hear again
The Buckeye Battle Cry.

Drive! Drive on down the field,
Men of the scarlet and gray;
Don't let them thru that line,
We have to win this game today,
Come on, Ohio!
Smash through to victory.
We cheer you as you go:
Our honor defend
So we'll fight to the end for O-hi-o.

Photo credit: Willy Chen

About the Author

Stephanie is from Sylvania, Ohio, and graduated from The Ohio State University in 2017 with an Early Childhood Education degree. In addition, she earned her Early Childhood Generalist Endorsement from Bowling Green State University and is enjoying her first year teaching for Sylvania City Schools. She enjoys going to football games at The Shoe, as well as cheering on the Buckeyes! While at Ohio State, she became involved in Ohio State University Women's Soccer Club, Chi Omega Fraternity, and was a Peer Leader for the office of First Year Experience. During her Early Childhood Education classes at Ohio State, she developed a passion for children's literature and created this story for a class project. She believes that everyone should find something they are passionate about because she has enjoyed the process of creating a children's book all about Ohio State game day. Creatively combining her two passions, the Buckeyes and children's literature, Stephanie is excited to share a spirited book that past, present, and future Buckeyes will enjoy for many years. The Ohio State University is the best school, and there's no better experience than being in Columbus on game day!

Have a book idea?

Contact us at:

info@mascotbooks.com | www.mascotbooks.com